TEXAS FOOTPRINTS

RITA KERR

EAKIN PRESS   ★   Austin, Texas

Published in the United States of America
By Eakin Press, P.O. Box 23069, Austin, Texas 78735

ISBN 0-89015-676-X

Library of Congress Cataloging-in-Publication Data

Kerr, Rita
    Texas footprints / Rita Kerr. — 1st ed.
        p.   cm. — (Stories for young Americans series)
    Summary: Relates the experiences of two young people growing up on the Texas frontier from their arrival with the first settlers from the United States in 1823 through the struggle for Texas independence.
        ISBN 0-89015-676-X : $8.95
    1. Texas — History — to 1846 — Juvenile fiction. [1. Texas — History — to 1846 — Fiction. 2. Frontier and pioneer life — Texas — Fiction.]
I. Title. II. Series.
PZ7.K468458Taj   1988
[Fic] — dc19   88-24299
                                                                  CIP
                                                                   AC

This book is dedicated to the memory of my great-great-grandparents, William Roberts and Elizabeth Pryor, who were true pioneers of early Texas. They came to Texas in 1823 as members of Stephen Austin's "Old Three Hundred" colonists, and in their way helped carve a great state out of a savage wilderness.

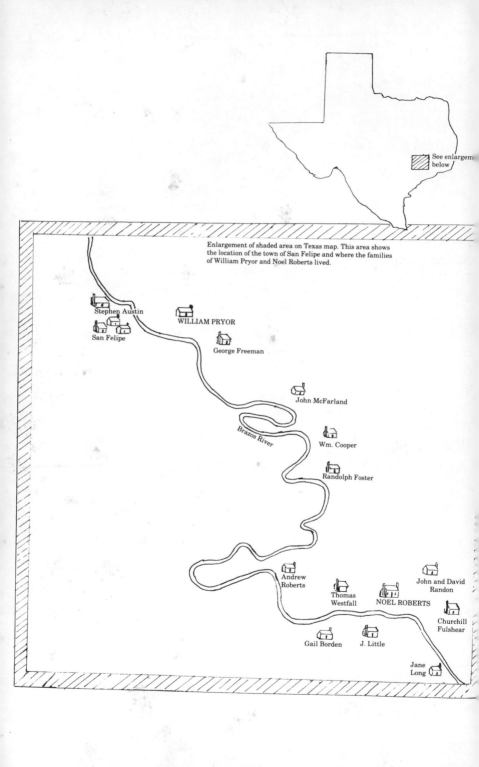

See enlargement below

Enlargement of shaded area on Texas map. This area shows the location of the town of San Felipe and where the families of William Pryor and Noel Roberts lived.

Stephen Austin

WILLIAM PRYOR

San Felipe

George Freeman

John McFarland

Brazos River

Wm. Cooper

Randolph Foster

Andrew Roberts

John and David Randon

Thomas Westfall

NOEL ROBERTS

Churchill Fulshear

Gail Borden

J. Little

Jane Long

Contents

Acknowledgments

The author wishes to thank the following people for their help and encouragement in writing *Texas Footprints:* Fern Dillard, Elizabeth Westberry, Carol Barclay, and Kitty Marosko. Special thanks to the many teachers and librarians for their interest in this book. The author's deepest thanks to the children who enjoy reading about life in early Texas.

Preface

In the year 1823, Stephen F. Austin received permission from the Mexican government to bring 300 families from the United States to Texas. The settlers in that first colony were known as the "Old Three Hundred." Ten-year-old William Roberts and five-year-old Elizabeth Pryor and their families were part of the "Old Three Hundred" pioneers.

Texas Footprints is the story of the adventures and hardships of those two young people as they grew older, fell in love, and were married. Together they faced floods, wild animals, and Indians, but their courage and determination helped to shape the destiny of Texas. When the Texas Revolution began, William fought in the Siege of Bexar and then in the Battle of San Jacinto.

The names of many of those first pioneers have been lost in the dusty pages of history. Now, in *Texas Footprints*, William Roberts and Elizabeth Pryor emerge to present a true story of the unsung heroes who devoted their lives to the making of Texas.

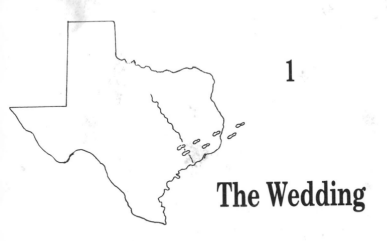

1

The Wedding

"Jumpin' catfish! What a wedding! William, do you think Stephen Austin will come?" Josiah exclaimed as he looked at his brother for an answer.

"He might. Most of the folks from San Felipe de Austin are here. Pa is pretty important in the town, isn't he?" William replied.

"Yep!"

"Are you sure Churchill brought enough cowbells?" Churchill was William's best friend. Josiah nodded. "Where did he hide them?"

"He put them over there," Josiah pointed to the clump of bushes near the cabin. "When are we going to start the racket?"

"It won't be long now. Mr. Smith, the *alcalde,* has finished the ceremony. Pa and Harriet are signing the marriage bond. Harriet's father, Mr. Pryor, has to sign it, too, and write the date — July 20, 1826. Then Pa will kiss his bride and shake hands with everybody."

"What for?" Josiah demanded.

His brother laughed. "How do I know? It's the custom. Maybe they are congratulating Pa for getting such a pretty young wife!"

Josiah's dark eyes flashed. "Maybe they are congratulating Harriet Pryor for marrying Pa! He is the smartest man in Texas! I'll bet that nobody has a house or farm as good as ours!"

"Now, Josiah, stop bragging." William knew that the other settlers along the Brazos River had the same rich, black land. "I have told you before that isn't the reason that Harriet is marrying Pa. Don't you understand? She likes Pa and a man needs a wife. Besides, you've heard Pa say that he needs a woman around the house to teach us manners."

"Humph! I don't see why. I think Pa has done a good job raising us since mama died back in Louisiana."

William nodded. "But Pa says it is time we had a mother."

"A mother?" Josiah scoffed in disgust. "How can Harriet Pryor be our mother? She is just four years older than you and six years older than me!"

"That's true. She is only seventeen."

"What kind of mother will she be?" Josiah complained.

"You might as well accept it. Pa thinks Harriet will make him a good wife. You behave yourself or I will fix you." His brother ducked as William playfully swung his fist in his direction. "Besides, we have to think of Pa. He isn't getting any younger!"

"He is not as old as Mr. Pryor, and I don't see *him* looking for a young wife."

"Maybe not," William agreed, "but with the shortage of women in Texas, I reckon Pa thinks he had better get a wife while he can."

The Roberts boys and their friends were standing on the porch near the cabin door. They watched the older folks shake hands with the groom and hug the bride. Widow Jane Long and her daughter, Ann, were among

2

the guests. Some of the people had come to Texas with William Pryor and Noel Roberts three years earlier, in 1823. Isaac Pennington, Randolph Foster, Soloman Williams, Rebecca Cummings, and the others had been part of Stephen Austin's first colony — the "Old Three Hundred."

Noel Roberts was a fine-looking man. He was taller than most — six foot — with black hair and dark, flashing eyes. William was proud when folks said he and Josiah looked like their father.

William looked at the young woman beside his father. Harriet Pryor glowed with excitement. She was wearing a garland of wildflowers in her long, brown hair. Her wedding dress was a simple blue calico that covered her from neck to toe.

Many of the guests shook hands with Harriet's father too. William Pryor was a rugged-looking man with iron-gray hair and beard. His calloused hands and weather-beaten skin were from years of hard work. From the happy expression on his face, there was little doubt the old man was proud of his daughter.

The bride's sisters were standing by their father. Mary was twenty and Elizabeth was eight. Mary also had long, brown hair and soft gray eyes. But the eight-year-old had yellow curls and big blue eyes.

"Hey, Josiah," William teased, "now you have a mother and two aunts!"

"Jumpin' catfish! Who needs aunts?"

The wedding party made its way to the refreshments spread on the hand-hewn table in the kitchen. There was smoked catfish, roasted deer, wild boar, turkey, and plenty of strong coffee for everyone. The meal was the best William Pryor could provide.

While the older guests were eating, the boys and younger children gathered in the yard. "Jumpin' catfish!" Josiah snickered. "I can't wait. A shivaree is the best part of any wedding!"

"Just be sure you don't make any noise until Churchill gives the signal," William warned as he helped his friend hand out the cowbells and sticks. "Everybody must act real innocent until it is time to start."

The boys hid the noisemakers behind them before they turned toward the house. Some of the older men were standing on the porch. When the bride and groom walked out the kitchen door, Churchill gave the signal.

"Shivaree! Shivaree!" everyone shouted at once.

BANG! RATTLE! BOOM!

The quiet evening was shattered with the ringing of cowbells, banging of pots, along with hooting and howling and all manner of deafening noises. The smaller children did their part by screaming and yelling as they chased each other around the porch. The shivaree went on and on until everyone grew weary.

When the racket died down, a gray-haired man began to play on his fiddle. The crowd moved aside to make room for the newlyweds to dance. As the fiddler tapped his foot and sawed out a tune on his fiddle, a man kept time with the music by banging on an iron triangle with a metal bar.

One by one the young people grabbed a partner to join in the fun. The older men were forced to move out into the yard to get away from the noise. They wanted to talk about the weather and their crops. While the young people were dancing, most of the wives gathered in the kitchen to share the latest gossip. A wedding was a special occasion for young and old alike.

The Pryor house, like most of the homes in Austin's colony, was a double cabin with an open breezeway porch. The house was made of rough, unhewn logs with a clapboard roof. Each room had a fireplace at one end. The furniture had been moved out of the larger cabin to make space for the dancers. The puncheon floor of rough wooden logs shook as the dancers stomped their feet. William Roberts and the other boys clustered around the doorway to watch. Some of them peered through the cracks between the logs.

4

"Hey, William," Daniel Shipman cried, "if you aren't going to dance, how about letting me borrow your hard-sole shoes? My feet will get full of splinters if I try to dance in these moccasins on that floor."

"Sure, Dan, you can borrow them."

Everyone knew Daniel had his eye set on Margarette Kelly. Of course, Daniel's feet were two sizes larger than William's. But he somehow managed to squeeze into William's shoes and limped onto the floor to dance with his girl. The other boys passed their shoes around. They did not want to miss out on the fun. Each time the music stopped, the couples stomped their feet and cheered until the fiddler struck up another tune. The young men and boys greatly outnumbered the unmarried ladies. If they wanted to dance, they were forced to ask the younger girls.

William saw that his friend Churchill was dancing with the youngest Pryor girl, Elizabeth. Her sister Mary was dancing with John Hensley. William punched his brother, "Josiah, now is your chance to dance with one of your new aunts."

"Jumpin' catfish! What for?"

"You want to welcome them into the family, don't you?"

"Humph!" Josiah snorted. "You dance with them. You're the oldest."

"All right, if you will let me wear your shoes. It looks like Daniel is going to dance in mine all night!"

Elizabeth smiled when William asked her to dance. With the first notes of the song "Cut the Pigeon's Wing," the two whirled around and around the room. The ruffles of Elizabeth's petticoats peeked from beneath her ankle-length dress as they danced. William caught sight of his father smiling in his direction. He smiled back.

"Thank you for the dance, Miss Pryor," William said politely when the music ended.

"Oh, call me Elizabeth," she said, pushing her sagging curls back from her face.

5

"We will probably be seeing a lot of each other now that your sister is married to my pa." As he looked down at her, William was silently noting how pretty she was. Elizabeth's blue eyes were the color of robin's eggs. The tiny freckles dotting her upturned nose looked like grains of sand. "Would you care to dance again?"

"I wish I could, but I promised the next one to Benjamin." Benjamin was Churchill's younger brother. Elizabeth's blue eyes twinkled merrily as she added, "Please ask me again."

Hours passed before William got another dance with her. It had not taken his friends long to discover that in spite of her age Elizabeth was a good dancer. Before the night was over, she had danced with most of the unmarried men and boys at the party.

While the young people enjoyed the music, the older guests grew weary. Most of them had talked until they were hoarse. The music and dancing went on and on. The fiddler played his last song as the morning sun came up over the tree tops. That was a signal to go home.

The families began to say goodbye and start for their wagons. Everyone laughed and cheered when Noel Roberts started off down the trail with his bride and his boys. Someone had tied the cowbells to the back of Noel's wagon. William and his brother sat in the back of the wagon with angelic looks on their faces. They thought the noise was funny. They were disappointed when their father insisted they remove the bells.

The last of the wedding guests waved farewell and headed for home. Elizabeth suddenly wanted to cry as she watched. Now that the party was over, everything seemed so quiet and lonely. She already missed her sister.

"Well," William Pryor sighed wearily as he put his arms around his daughters, "time is wasting. Come along. I want my breakfast. I have work to do."

6

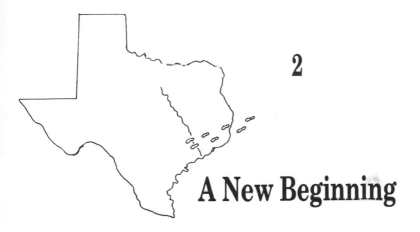

2

A New Beginning

"Well, my dear," Noel Roberts said as he watched his bride from the doorway, "do you think you'll be happy here?"

"Oh, yes! Your house is bigger than I remembered."

Noel laughed. "That isn't surprising. After all, you were here only once with your papa. The rooms are somewhat larger than you are used to. Since I had plenty of trees and two strong boys to help me, we took our time building this kitchen. We started the other room once we had the corn planted. In fact, we just finished the loft out on the porch. The boys like sleeping up there."

Harriet turned around slowly to study the room. "Goodness! I'll bet you could cook enough food for an army in that fireplace!"

"It is large. And you will find that we *do* like to eat," Noel said with a twinkle in his eyes. "The boys are always hungry. I trust you enjoy cooking."

Harriet nodded. She only hoped they liked her cooking. She had never cooked for two boys before. Noel kissed her as he went out to unhitch the wagon. While he was gone, Harriet cooked their breakfast. Cornbread and mush were on the table when they returned. She waited to pour the coffee until they were seated. The new bride picked at her food, afraid they would not like what she had fixed. She finally decided they were satisfied from the way the boys bolted it down.

Noel told his wife that he and the boys were going hunting. With the shortage of ammunition, Josiah could only practice shooting at a moving object. Noel said they would return with a rabbit or — with luck — a deer.

"By the way," Noel went on, "if you care to look, you might find some vegetables in the garden to cook for supper. You can get acquainted with your new home while we are gone. If you are tired you may take a nap."

"A nap? What for?" Harriet exclaimed in surprise. "I'm not sick."

"I know that," Noel chuckled. "But we danced most of the night. And, with all the excitement, you must be tired. Isn't that right, boys?"

"Yep!" Josiah mumbled.

"Sure is," William agreed with a sleepy yawn. "You and Pa danced almost as much as I did. Before the night was over my feet felt like they were going to fall off. Josiah's shoes were too tight. Dan had mine."

"We'll be on our way," Noel said, rising from the table.

The boys picked up their guns and headed for the door. "See you later," William called back over his shoulder. Noel kissed Harriet and followed them outside.

Harriet hummed a tune as she busied herself in the kitchen. When she finished, she picked up the bucket and went to the garden.

There were plenty of beans for supper. The peas and squashes were almost ripe. She could use those for another meal. She grabbed a handful of wild garlic to season the beans and noticed a patch of berries still too green to pick. Returning to the kitchen, she took one of

8

the chairs to the breezeway. Then she opened the doors between the two rooms before she sat down to shell the beans. From the porch she could see everything in the house and around the yard.

It was not often Harriet had time to think about the past. As she shelled the beans, she let her mind drift back to those last days in Alabama . . .

Back in 1821, Papa had heard folks talking about Stephen Austin. Austin had received a grant from the Mexican government to take 300 families to Texas to start a colony. Harriet remembered her father saying to her mother, "Life has not been easy. It was bad when we lived in Tennessee with Mary and little Harriet. We had hoped life would be better here in Alabama, but now we are having trouble scratching out a living."

Harriet's mother had said, "These are just hard times, William."

"I know, but we have to think of the girls. Perhaps we should join Austin's group going to Texas, Beth. I understand there's plenty of good, rich land and beautiful streams of water. They say herds of buffalo and horses run wild on the broad prairies. Texas might be just the place for us. You know it won't be many years before the girls will be settling down with their own families. We have to plan for the future, Beth."

They had talked and talked about Texas. Finally, Papa settled the matter. They were moving! They loaded the covered wagon with all it would hold and joined the other settlers.

Harriet had nothing but unhappy memories of that journey. It was awful. The weather turned cold. The rains came. The trails were knee-deep in mud. More than once their heavy wagon got stuck. Everyone had worked to get it out. Several other wagons had to be unpacked to get them unstuck.

With the heavy rains, many of the rivers overflowed their banks. When Harriet closed her eyes, she could still see little Elizabeth clinging to her mother when the wagons were carried across the rushing waters on rafts or flat-bottom barges.

A number of people got sick. Harriet's mother was one of them. Before they reached Texas, she came down with chills and a high fever. Harriet had nightmares of the dreadful night Ma took a turn for the worse. She and her sisters spent the night in another wagon while some of the women tried to help Ma. There was nothing they could do.

The next morning, an eerie silence fell upon the camp. Everyone spoke in hushed whispers and, with downcast eyes, walked around shaking their heads. Harriet knew something was wrong before Papa took her into his arms and told them the awful news. Their mother had died. Harriet would never forget that day. They buried their mother beside the trail.

The rest of the journey was like a bad dream. Mary tried to take her mother's place, but no one could. After the wagons rolled into Texas it seemed they would never stop. But they did. Someone said the town of San Felipe de Austin would be built on that very spot.

Harriet's father was not concerned about a town. He wanted to find a piece of land that would suit their needs. He picked a site on the east side of the Brazos River next to Stephen Austin's land and went to work. Chopping trees and notching the logs for a house was not easy. Harriet and her sisters tried to help, but there was not much they could do.

The one-room house they built had no windows or floor. Papa said those would come later. Crude as it was, the cabin was more comfortable than living in the crowded wagon. Harriet hated that wagon. It would always remind her of her mother's death.

Mosquitoes and gnats came in through the cracks between the logs of the house. The girls tried to fill the cracks with mud, but it did not keep out the bugs. The mosquitoes were bad in the daytime. At night they were awful. Papa put up netting to keep the insects from eating them alive during the night.

Once the cabin was finished, it was time to plant the corn. Corn was their main food. Like the other settlers, they ate it boiled and fried and roasted. Mary made mush, hominy, grits, and bread with corn. When the girls complained, their father said, "Remember, anything will taste good if you are hungry. We should thank the good Lord we've got it. And, of course, give thanks for the cow that gives us milk for this butter."

Some of the settlers had brought slaves to Texas. They also brought cotton. And they soon learned that cotton grew well in Texas.

Harriet was concerned because her father worked so hard. He was in the field from dawn until dusk. When he came home in the evenings, he had blisters on his hands from chopping trees and pulling weeds. Mary sometimes worked at her father's side. She wore a wide-brimmed bonnet and a long-sleeved dress to protect her skin from the blistering sun. But she turned brown and freckled anyway. The other women who worked in the fields got sunburned too.

Mary insisted that her younger sisters learn to sew and cook the way their mother had taught her. She kept saying, "Someday you will get married and have girls you will have to teach." Harriet always thought that sounded silly. Now that she was married, she thought differently.

With so much work to be done, everyone had a job. Papa made sure there was plenty of wood for the fireplace. Elizabeth was to help with the dishes and churn the butter. Harriet filled the buckets with water and helped Mary with the cooking.

Every Monday, Papa built a fire in the yard and brought water for the washing. The girls had to keep the fire going to get the water hot enough to wash the clothes. They took turns sloshing them up and down with a long stick to loosen the dirt. Once everything was clean and rinsed, the clothes were spread over the bushes to dry. Tuesday was the day they ironed. It was a chore they did not enjoy. The flat iron was heavy and had to be reheated many times. The girls looked forward to Wednesday. They would not have to wash and iron for a whole week!

One day Mary found a precious treasure in the family trunk. It was a small bundle of garden seeds that had been tucked in the folds of her mother's wedding dress. With their father's help, the girls dug holes in the ground and buried the tiny seeds. What fun they had watching the plants shoot up! Harriet had wonderful memories of their first delicious meal of turnips and peas from that garden . . .

"Mercy!" Harriet exclaimed, shaking her head. "I must have been daydreaming! What on earth will Noel think of me? I guess Papa was right when he said there is no need looking back. Life goes on. Those days are gone forever."

And life did go on. Harriet was happy in her new home. But, without her sisters to help, she learned that a woman's work was never done. It seemed that she finished cooking one meal only in time to start another. William and Josiah liked her cooking, but she had no idea that two boys could eat so much. Harriet did not mind preparing the food, but she grew weary of cleaning the kitchen. To make matters worse, there was always washing and ironing to do. She was used to washing and ironing for her father, but now she had to wash for three men. Their pants were not only heavy but hard to handle when soaking wet. Ironing their things was not easy either.

Harriet felt that life was somehow easier for men. They did not seem to work all the time. They could go hunting and fishing after their chores were done. Sometimes Noel and the boys returned with a deer or a wild hog with sharp tusks. At night they sat around talking about their adventures. If the boys were lucky, they would find a bee tree loaded with wild honey. Harriet wondered if anything exciting ever happened in a woman's life.

One evening, after they had been married about a month, Noel said, "You mentioned that we were almost out of coffee. Do we need anything else?"

"We could use some salt."

"How would you like to visit your folks? You haven't been home since the wedding."

"Go home? Oh, could I?" Harriet cried excitedly.

"I don't see why not. I need to pick up some supplies and get the plow fixed — the point is broken. The boys will have to take it in the wagon. You and I can ride Blacky, the bay-colored horse. I will leave you at your father's house on my way to town and come back for you later. Would you like that?" Harriet surprised him by throwing her arms around his neck.

"Oh, you are so thoughtful. I would love to see my family. I want to tell them how happy I am and how wonderful you are!"

3

A Visit

"My, it's good to be home!" Harriet said as Noel rode off toward town. "I didn't know I was so homesick to see you."

"I figured it was about time you paid us a visit, daughter." William Pryor peered at her closely. "There isn't anything wrong, is there?"

"No, Papa!" Harriet laughed. "Noel was going to San Felipe for supplies and he brought me along. The boys took the wagon. Wasn't Noel thoughtful to ask if you needed anything from Davis's store before he left?"

"Sure was. He saved me a trip to town."

Elizabeth clung to her sister muttering, "You did come home! You did come home!"

"You can see how much we've missed you," Mary said, squeezing Harriet's hand.

"And I have missed you. Papa, are you all right? You're not working too hard, are you? You look tired."

"No, daughter, hard work never hurt a fellow." Her father sighed deeply, adding, "But the work is never

14

done. In fact, the field is waiting for me right now. I will be back at noon. We can visit then." He smashed his battered hat onto his head and headed out the door.

"Papa's right. The work is never done. I had better finish making the butter." Elizabeth ran to her stool by the wooden churn.

Mary held her sister at arm's length. "Married life must agree with you. You are pretty as a picture!"

"Oh, Mary," Harriet laughed.

"Well, I've made up my mind. I will never get married!" Elizabeth cried unexpectedly. "I am going to be an old maid!"

Her sister chuckled. "I recall I felt that way when I was eight years old. But when you are older, Betsy, you will change your mind."

"Never! Besides, I will be nine on my birthday."

Harriet brushed the curl from her forehead and said, "Don't say never. By the time you're seventeen you will want a home and children of your own. Just wait and see."

No one spoke. The only sound in the kitchen was that of the cream sloshing from side to side as Elizabeth plunged the dasher up and down. "I will never leave Papa! Who would make the butter and set the table for him?"

Her older sister smiled. "You are right, Betsy. Papa does need you. And so do I."

A frown crossed Elizabeth's face. She thought of Harriet's words. "Does Papa look tired? Is he all right? What if he got sick like Ma did? What would we do?"

"Now, Betsy, don't worry. Noel and I would be here in no time if anything was wrong. We are not far away."

"Harriet," the girl stopped her churning to stare at her, "do you love Noel Roberts?"

"Betsy! What a question!" Harriet exclaimed in surprise.

"Well, do you?"

Her sister gazed at the floor thoughtfully. "Well . . . I

15

do not love him the way I do you or Mary or Papa. I love Noel in a different way. It is hard to explain. I know I will make him a good wife."

With her blue eyes flashing, Elizabeth shook her finger. "You just wait, Harriet! You will get so busy washing clothes and cleaning house and being a mother to those boys, you will forget about us! I won't ever get to see you." She suddenly burst into tears and buried her head in her hands.

Harriet hurried across the room to clasp the child to her bosom. She understood Elizabeth's feelings.

With her sister's arms around her, Elizabeth thought of the things that had happened. It seemed all the trouble began when they started for Texas. She, too, had unpleasant memories of that trip. She remembered being cold and wet and miserable. Nothing had seemed right since her mother's death. Those memories filled Elizabeth's head as her sister tried to comfort her.

"Please don't cry, Betsy," Harriet whispered, stroking Elizabeth's curls. Suddenly, she had an idea. "Would you like to go home with me?"

"Go home with you?" Elizabeth asked.

"Noel will be back this way with the wagon. He will have to bring the things Papa wanted from town. You could ride home with William and Josiah in the wagon." Harriet's eyes sparkled with excitement as she talked.

"Oh, could I, Mary?" Elizabeth waited breathlessly for an answer.

"I don't know. You'll have to ask Papa," Mary replied.

"Don't worry, Betsy. I'll talk to him when he comes in. Say . . . what time is it? We must get busy. Papa will be hungry when he comes home." Harriet knew it would never do for him to catch them wasting time. It was like old times as the three worked to get the meal on the table.

While Papa was eating, Harriet did a lot of talking. Her father finally agreed Elizabeth could go for a four-day visit. Harriet was afraid to ask for a longer visit for fear Papa would change his mind.

It did not take Elizabeth long to get ready. When Noel returned he was pleased that Elizabeth was going home with them. After they unloaded Mr. Pryor's supplies, Noel put Elizabeth's bundle of clothes in the back of the wagon beside Josiah. By putting her foot on the wheel, Elizabeth managed to pull herself into the wagon. She sat on the seat by William. Noel mounted his horse and took Harriet's hand to help her up onto the saddle behind him. With everyone shouting goodbyes at once, they were off.

Elizabeth leaned against the wagon, waving her arms as long as she could see Mary flapping her apron. With a heavy sigh, Elizabeth sat down. "I can't believe I am really going," she said as she smoothed her petticoats and skirt over her high-topped shoes.

"Yes, but your sister had to promise that you would be home by dark on Friday," William answered. "You must be a hard worker. Your papa kept saying, 'There's work to do.' "

Elizabeth giggled. "Oh, he is always saying that." She looked back at Josiah. He was leaning against the supply sacks with a blade of grass between his teeth. His head rested on one arm while he stared at the cloudless August sky. "Are you comfortable?"

"Yep!"

Elizabeth could think of nothing more to say. William chuckled softly. "Don't mind him. He never talks much until he gets to know you. Pa says I talk enough for both of us. And I reckon I do."

"I like to talk, but nobody listens most of the time. Say, how far is it to your place?"

"Well," William scratched his head thoughtfully, "going up the Brazos River by boat it would probably be about twenty miles or more. But by land it's about twelve miles — maybe thirteen. A fellow on horseback could make it in a couple of hours or less."

17

As they rode along, William talked about the trees. He pointed out the oak, elm, and cottonwood, as well as the pecan and cypress growing by the creeks and river. Elizabeth had not noticed the thick buffalo grass or the chocolate brown dirt until he mentioned them. She found it easy to talk to William, but Josiah was different. Since she had no brothers, Elizabeth had not been around many boys. Her sisters were her best friends.

"You know, the Brazos River is too deep and swift for a wagon to cross without Mr. McFarland's ferry boat," William said. "It is interesting how he stretches two ropes across the river and ties one of the ropes to a big tree. He uses the other rope to pull his boat across the river."

Elizabeth nodded. "Papa says we could not get along without the ferry."

"And every time we go to San Felipe it has changed. My pa says it is strange that the town has a tavern and a saloon but no church. We heard that Isaac Pennington plans to open a school before long."

"That's good," Elizabeth replied. She watched the horses swish their tails from side to side to brush away the flies. "Mama wanted Harriet and me to go to school, but Papa never had the money to send us."

"Don't feel badly. I never had a chance to go to school either. Pa says there were lots of folks who had to sign their land grants with an X because they couldn't write their names." William was eager to change the subject. He was embarrassed that he could not read or write, but he pretended he did not care. "Say, do you like horses?"

"Yes, but I don't know how to ride very well. Papa never has time to teach me. After working all week he is too tired on Sunday. He says that's a day of rest."

William thought it strange she did not know how to ride. He had been riding a horse for as long as he could remember. "Hey, maybe I could give you a lesson or two while you are visiting. Old Red — she is that

18

chestnut-colored horse on the right — is real gentle. Isn't she, Josiah?"

"Yep," Josiah said. "I figured it was about time we got home."

Two black dogs ran to meet them as William slowed the wagon. "Buelah, you and Sam stop barking," William scolded as he stopped in front of the cabin. He helped Elizabeth to the ground and handed her the bundle of clothes. She followed her sister into the house while the boys helped their father unload the supplies.

"Oh, Betsy," Harriet cried, squeezing her hand, "I am so glad you are here. I know we will have fun. Are you hungry?"

Elizabeth nodded her head. "I guess I am."

"I thought we would have fish. It won't take the boys long to catch enough for supper. Why don't you run along with them? While you are gone, I will build the fire and make the cornbread. Is it all right if Betsy goes fishing with you, Josiah?"

"Yep!" Josiah said. "Come on."

The boys took their fishing poles from the porch and headed for the river. The bank was cool from the shade of the pecan and cypress trees. The fish started biting as soon as the boys had their lines in the water. They soon had enough catfish for supper. Elizabeth was glad. The mosquitoes were biting her fiercely. Harriet was ready to fry the cleaned fish when they got home. Everyone was hungry.

The next morning Noel reminded the boys that the three of them were going to the field to finish picking the corn. William winked at Elizabeth as he said, "Pa, before we go, I want to ask you a question. Is it all right if I give Elizabeth a riding lesson this evening? She doesn't know how to ride."

"Oh, please, Mr. Roberts," Elizabeth pleaded.

"I don't see why not." Noel smiled down at her. "But, child, you can't go on calling me Mr. Roberts. The boys

19

call me Pa. You can call me Pa if you want to. I always wanted a pretty, blonde-headed, blue-eyed daughter."

Even Josiah laughed as they picked up their guns and headed for the door.

The girls spent the day sewing and cooking. As they worked, Elizabeth kept thinking of riding Old Red. That evening after supper, William saddled up the horses. Harriet helped by holding the reins so Noel could lift Elizabeth into the saddle.

"Now, remember," Noel said, "to go say 'giddup.' She will stop if you say 'whoa.' Old Red usually listens real good. That is more than I can say about the boys." Elizabeth saw the twinkle in Noel's eyes as he handed her the reins.

William mounted his horse and looked over at Elizabeth. "Are you comfortable?"

Elizabeth nodded her head. She wanted to laugh at his question. How could she be comfortable with her skirts above her shoes and her feet dangling crazily in the air? Her legs were too short to reach the stirrups, but she was too excited to notice.

"Real slow now, Old Red, giddup," William commanded. The horse obeyed. William instructed Elizabeth to pull the reins first to the right and then to the left. The horse stopped as she pulled back on the reins. When William felt that Elizabeth knew what she was doing, he told her they would walk the horses over to the trees.

"Oh, this is fun," Elizabeth cried as they rode along.

William pushed the black hair back from his forehead and laughed. After they had ridden side by side a short distance, he said, "We'll go a little faster. Come on, Old Red, let's go." William gave his own horse a gentle nudge. Away he went. Old Red was not far behind.

Elizabeth felt she was flying as she bounced up and down in the saddle. Her bonnet slid from her head and dangled halfway down her back. She was too happy to care. She was riding a horse all by herself!

William swerved his horse to miss some thorny

As William's horse emerged from the trees he saw Old Red bolting toward the house with Elizabeth hanging on for dear life.

bushes and rode into a grove of trees. He disappeared from sight. Elizabeth had been daydreaming. Surprised to find him gone, she became confused about how to pull the reins. Without realizing what she was doing, she pulled in the wrong direction. That caused Old Red to brush against the thorny bushes. The horse felt the sharp needles scrape against her legs and panicked. She wheeled around and headed for home on the run. Elizabeth grabbed the saddle to keep from falling. She tried to scream but could make no sound.

When William realized that Old Red was not behind him, he rode back to find her. As his horse emerged from the trees, he saw Old Red bolting toward the house with Elizabeth hanging on for dear life. Little by little, his horse gained on Old Red. As William came alongside he caught the reins. "Whoa, Old Red, whoa," he called loudly. The mare slowed her pace and came to a stop. "Are you all right, Betsy?"

Elizabeth swallowed the lump in her throat. "Yes . . . but I was so scared. Thank you for saving me."

William breathed a sigh of relief. "I'm sure glad you weren't hurt. I think you have learned enough for today. We had better say nothing about this. It is good they couldn't see us from the house. Pa might not let me give you another lesson. Shall we call this our little secret?"

Elizabeth nodded and smiled.

Friday came all too soon. Elizabeth wondered how time could pass so quickly. She had worked with Harriet, but it had been fun. The best part of her visit was riding Old Red and getting to know William. But now it was over. Noel and William were taking her home that afternoon. Josiah was staying behind with Harriet.

While the horses were being saddled, Harriet made a bundle of Elizabeth's clothes. Harriet was already making plans for her sister's next visit. The girls were waiting on the porch when Noel returned with the horses.

"William wanted to ride Blacky so you can ride with him," Noel explained. He took Elizabeth by the waist and lifted her into the saddle behind his son. "Now hold William around the waist so you won't fall off."

"I will hold on," Elizabeth promised.

"We should be back before dark," Noel said as he kissed his wife. Blacky pawed the ground impatiently. Noel took his long rifle in his hand and mounted his horse.

"I have had a wonderful time. Goodbye," Elizabeth cried back over her shoulder.

"Betsy, be sure to thank Papa for letting you come. I will see you soon. Goodbye!" Harriet and Josiah watched them ride away.

William and his father talked loudly in order for Elizabeth to hear. They showed her places where the Brazos River twisted and curved like a snake through Randolph Foster's land. About a mile further down the road they came to William Cooper's place. His fields were white with cotton. When they rode by, the cotton pickers looked up and waved. They waved back. The workers sang while they worked. Elizabeth could still hear them long after they were out of sight. William called her attention to several buzzards circling and spiraling down to the ground to where a dead animal lay. The birds flew into a nearby tree when the riders came nearer. Elizabeth noticed a dead deer beside the trail.

Seeing the deer reminded William of the first buck he had shot when he was ten years old. He said that Josiah was nine when he killed his first deer. When Elizabeth told him she did not know how to load or shoot a gun, William promised to teach her. His father agreed that with the danger of wild animals and snakes, every woman and child should know how to shoot a gun. William noticed that his father did not mention the danger of Indians.

With so much to see and talk about, Elizabeth lost track of time. She was surprised to see they were passing their neighbor George Freeman's place. That meant she was home!

Mary ran into the yard when she heard them. "Oh, my, you are early! Papa didn't expect you so soon. Come on in and sit a spell, Mr. Roberts. Papa should be home before long. He is clearing some land down by the river."

"I wish we could stay, Mary, but I promised Harriet we would be back before dark. We'll need to stop at the river for the horses to drink. We'll see your papa there." As he talked, Noel was helping Elizabeth to the ground. "Well, young lady, you are home safe and sound. You must come and visit us again. We enjoyed having you."

"I truly had a good time," Elizabeth said. "Goodbye."

"Goodbye, Betsy. Remember we will go hunting the next time you come." William's voice faded into the distance.

Elizabeth was eager to tell Mary about her visit, but she continued waving until William and his father were out of sight.

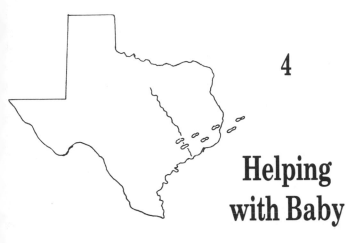

4

Helping
with Baby

The months that followed were busy. The next time she visited her sister, Elizabeth was pleased that William remembered his promise to teach her how to shoot a gun.

William showed her how to pour the powder from the powder horn and pack it down into the musket. He warned her not to touch the trigger until she was ready to fire. After she had learned the parts of the gun and how to load it, William said she was ready to go hunting. She would have to learn to shoot at a moving target. Ammunition was too dear to waste.

Early the next morning, just after daybreak, they rode down to the river. Josiah and the two dogs went too. They tied their horses to a tree and walked down to the river bank. There they hid behind a clump of bushes. William had warned that the smallest noise could frighten away any creature coming to drink. He told the dogs to sit and held onto them to be sure they did not get in the way. They had not been there long when a fierce-looking wild pig, a javelina boar, with long tusks appeared.

"Shh," William whispered softly. "That pig is dangerous. He could kill one of these dogs or you with those tusks. Wait until I give the signal, then shoot! If by chance he is just wounded, be ready to run! An injured animal sometimes goes mad."

"That's a cheerful thought," Elizabeth muttered to herself. Tense with excitement and fear, she held her breath as they waited. The javelina slowly turned its head and looked around. Elizabeth feared it might hear the pounding of her heart. When the creature lowered its head into the water, William raised his hand. That was the signal to get ready. Elizabeth and Josiah raised their guns.

"Fire!" William commanded. BANG! Their shots echoed through the still morning air. The pig threw back its head, rolling its eyes wildly from side to side. With a loud grunt it turned as if to run, then stopped. The javelina swayed back and forth before it slumped to the ground. With a quiver and a moan, it lay still. "Come on! He's dead," William said, getting to his feet.

"I got him! I got him!" Elizabeth cried, jumping up and down excitedly. The dogs raced to the javelina and sniffed around to be sure it was dead.

"Humph!" Josiah scoffed. "I shot him!"

They saw a hole in the pig's chest and another one through the right ear. Josiah swore his shot killed the animal. Elizabeth vowed it was hers. The argument was never settled.

Before Elizabeth returned home from that trip, Harriet asked her if she would like one of Buelah and Sam's puppies. They were due any day. Her sister reminded her that she would have to get Papa's permission. When Elizabeth got home she asked her father. He shook his head — "no." She reminded him that a dog could warn them of danger. Papa finally agreed she could have one if she

26

Elizabeth held her breath as they waited for William's signal to shoot. She feared the javelina might hear the banging of her heart.

promised to return it if the puppy was not a good watch dog. She promised.

On Elizabeth's next visit, Buelah was proud to show off her puppies. Harriet told Elizabeth she could have her pick of the litter, but she could not take the puppy home until it was weaned. Elizabeth had a hard time deciding. She wanted them all. She finally settled on one of the two fat, roly-poly puppies with black and white paws. William picked the other as his. He suggested that Elizabeth call hers Rex and he would name his Tex. Elizabeth hated going home without Rex.

When the puppy was eight weeks old, William put him in a leather pouch and tied a string loosely around his neck. He laid the dog across the saddle to take him to Elizabeth. The puppy cried and whined most of the way. When William reached Elizabeth's house, he lifted Rex out of the bag and put him on the ground. The puppy staggered around to get his balance. He ate a few bites of food and then crawled up into Elizabeth's lap and went to sleep. They feared that the bouncy trip had been too much for the puppy. But when Rex awoke, he was ready to play.

The dog liked Elizabeth's father. He soon followed Papa everywhere. He barked at everything that moved, even his shadow. Papa seemed satisfied that Rex would make a good watch dog. They would keep him. The puppy thought he belonged to Papa. Elizabeth did not see much of Rex after that.

Harriet and Noel had been married about a year when little Elisha was born. One of their neighbors, Rebecca Cummings, stayed with Harriet for a few days after the baby arrived.

Like all proud fathers, Noel was eager to brag about his new son. He and William rode to the Pryor house to share the news. Before they left, Noel asked Mary if she would go back with him. Elizabeth spoke up, "Let me go. I can cook. I'm as strong as Mary. I'm almost ten, you know. I can help Harriet with the baby." Elizabeth

Elizabeth had difficulty selecting a puppy.

pleaded with her sister. "Please, Mary, let me go. You stay home with Papa. He needs you." Everyone finally agreed that Elizabeth could go in Mary's place.

Elizabeth fell in love with the baby. Elisha had dark black hair and dimpled cheeks. Elizabeth never knew anything so tiny could be so much trouble. Elisha was always wet or hungry — or both. With a new baby, there was no time for Elizabeth to go hunting or fishing on that trip.

After the baby's arrival, Elizabeth's visits with Harriet grew longer and longer. One day Harriet said, "I am grateful you want to stay with us, Betsy. I really don't know how we would get along without you."

The baby whimpered softly in his sleep. Elizabeth gave the cradle a gentle rock as she whispered, "I guess we need each other."

As time passed, there were many changes in Texas. When Elizabeth was at home she listened to her father talk about the new law the Mexican government had passed. The law meant no more settlers would be allowed to come to Texas from the States. Some of their neighbors thought the law was unfair. They had friends and relatives who wanted to move to Texas. With the new law, they would be unable to come. Elizabeth's father was also unhappy when he learned that the government had sent soldiers to some of the forts in the eastern part of Texas. There was talk of the settlers losing their rights. Her father said that something had to be done before that happened. Many people agreed. They decided to have a meeting to discuss the problem.

The settlers met at San Felipe that spring of 1833. Most were proud of being loyal citizens of Mexico. They obeyed the laws, but they wanted separate statehood. They felt the capital of the province should be moved from Saltillo. That town was too far away. Some did not think Texas should remain part of the province of Coahuila. Others talked of having their own government and of making their own laws.

One of the delegates was a man from Tennessee named Sam Houston. Before the meeting adjourned, the members adopted a state constitution. Sam Houston helped them write the constitution. He also helped them make a list of their requests to send to the government. They asked Stephen Austin to take the requests to Mexico City. He agreed to do so.

When Austin presented the paper to the Mexican officials, they were not pleased with the settlers' demands. Austin decided to meet with General Antonio López de Santa Anna, the new president of Mexico, hoping that he would agree to the demands. It was months before Austin could talk to the president. When they did meet, Santa Anna agreed to change the law and let settlers come into Texas. The capital was moved from Saltillo to Monclova. But the president would not allow Texas to form a separate provincial government.

With his mission completed, Stephen Austin started home. He never reached Texas. Austin was arrested and returned to Mexico City. He was placed in a dark, damp prison and forced to remain there for more than a year. When the settlers learned of his imprisonment, they asked that Stephen Austin be freed. They were ignored.

The settlers, who called themselves Texans, had hoped Santa Anna would be a good president. They soon discovered he meant to rule with an iron hand. He assumed complete control of the government. Everyone was concerned. Many of the citizens of Mexican descent living in Texas worried about the future of Texas.

Elizabeth did not understand it all, but she had a feeling there was going to be trouble.

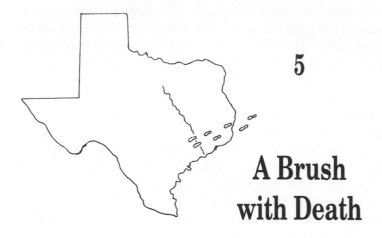

5

A Brush with Death

By mid-1833 the town of San Felipe had two hotels, a blacksmith shop, over thirty houses, and a number of stores. It also had a newspaper, the *Texas Gazette*. By that time, the Mexicans living in Texas were greatly outnumbered by the Anglo-Americans. More than 3,000 people lived in Austin's colony.

There were other colonies in Texas too. Green DeWitt brought more than 100 families and started a settlement at Gonzales. Martín de León settled near the coast with some 200 families. Each settlement had its own capital. Elizabeth heard of towns like San Antonio, Gonzales, Victoria, and Brazoria. Many of the original problems still remained for the newcomers to Texas. They faced wild animals and hostile Indians.

With their cabins finished and their crops planted, the people had more time for social gatherings. Sunday became their day for visiting. Folks thought nothing of traveling ten or twelve miles to attend a picnic or party. Dances and quilting parties were special occasions. The men went hunting and fishing while the ladies had their quilting bees. When the women gathered around the quilt to sew, the children played games of tag or hide-and-seek. Those parties gave Elizabeth a chance to be with other girls her age. William enjoyed them because he could visit with Churchill Fulshear and his friends. Elizabeth noticed Josiah even liked the parties.

Elizabeth visited her sister whenever she had the chance. Harriet now had two small children. She needed help. But when Elizabeth was away from home for very long, she worried about her father. The years of hard work had aged him. Papa could no longer work from dawn to dusk the way he had when they first came to Texas. She realized he was spending more and more time dozing in his rocker, with Rex at his feet.

One morning in June, Elizabeth stood at the window, shaking her head. "It is still raining! Won't it ever stop, Papa? It has rained for days."

"Just be thankful we live up here on high ground and not down on the river bottom," her father reminded her. "Think of those who live on Oyster Creek. If the Brazos gets much higher they will have trouble. We should pray for them."

"You are so right, Papa," Mary agreed. "I am just grateful that Noel's house is on high ground too."

"I keep thinking about Harriet." Elizabeth turned from the window to look at her father. "If it stops raining, may I go see her?"

"Child," her father explained patiently, "we have been over this before. I have told you it is not safe to travel alone."

"Oh, Papa! I am not a child. I am fourteen . . . I will be fifteen on my birthday in October."

William Pryor shook his head. Elizabeth's mother Beth had been fifteen the day he married her. Elizabeth was like her mother in many ways. She had Beth's soft blue eyes and rosebud lips, along with her blonde wavy hair and upturned nose. Elizabeth even walked and talked like Beth. Her father was reminded of a caterpillar changing into a butterfly as he watched Elizabeth blossom into womanhood. She became more beautiful each day. From the gleam in William Roberts's eyes, there was little doubt that he admired Elizabeth too.

William Pryor worried as he looked at his oldest daughter, Mary. Texas had not been kind to her, he thought. She appeared older than her twenty-seven years. But John Hensley did not seem to notice. John had become a regular visitor. It was just a matter of time before he asked Mary to be his wife. William muttered softly, "That is the way the good Lord planned it. A time to work, a time to wed, a time to die."

The rains continued through the month of June. The river overflowed, uprooting trees and bushes along the way. Crossing the swollen Brazos to get to town on the ferry boat was impossible. The men on the east bank used many excuses to get out of their homes for a while. Facing the rain was somehow better than being trapped indoors with the women and a bunch of unruly children all day.

Rumors flew when the men got together. It was said that two of William Little's servants and most of his animals had washed away. William Little and his son Walter were part of Austin's "Old Three Hundred" colonists who lived downstream. One neighbor said a number of folks had been forced from their homes by the high water. Rumor also had it that one man had been caught in the swift current. He managed to grab hold of a cedar tree to keep from drowning. The man spent the night swaying back and forth on a limb over the swirling waters. After listening to their tales, William Pryor vowed he would build an ark if it kept on raining.

The skies cleared the first day of July. The sun finally came out. As the waters receded, the fields were left knee-deep in mud. The farmers soon discovered their cotton and corn seeds had rotted in the ground. That meant there would be a shortage of corn by fall.

Although the rains were over, there was another worry — mosquitoes. Swarms of them! Papa swore some were as big as grasshoppers. Elizabeth had to agree that they were big and fierce. During the hot, humid days the mosquitoes made life unbearable. The nights were worse.

The people soon had a new fear. An epidemic of yellow fever hit the colony. It spread from home to home, touching family after family with frightening speed. Age was no barrier. From the onset of chills and fever, the disease acted quickly on young and old alike. By the time the epidemic reached its peak, there were many new graves. Toward the end of August it appeared the worst of the epidemic was over. Elizabeth thought death had passed them by. She was wrong.

One morning her father complained of being cold. His teeth were chattering. To her dismay, Elizabeth found he had a burning fever. In spite of his protests, they got Papa to bed and covered him with quilts. They were heating the flat irons to wrap in cloths to warm his feet when Rex started barking. Someone rode into the yard. It was Papa's young red-headed friend from South Carolina, William Barret Travis. Mr. Travis was one of several lawyers who had set up offices in San Felipe. When Elizabeth told him of her father's illness, Mr. Travis promised to get word to her sister.

Harriet and Noel were there before the day was over. Elizabeth felt better knowing that William had come along. They did what they could, but poor Papa was beyond their help. There was no medicine or earthly cure for yellow fever. The next morning, after a sleepless night, the family gathered around the old man's bed. He opened his eyes and looked from one to another. A faint smile slipped across his face when he saw Elizabeth. His eyelids fluttered and, with a heavy sigh, he was gone.

Elizabeth sank to her knees beside his bed sobbing, "Papa, Papa."

Noel tried to comfort her while William rode to the neighbors to tell them of William Pryor's death. The next morning, September 10, a number of people, including William Travis and John Hensley, came to the funeral. Elizabeth felt sure that Stephen Austin would have been there had he not been in a Mexican jail.

That afternoon, John Hensley took Mary aside. After a short talk, they announced they were getting married. Out of respect for her father, Mary insisted on a quiet ceremony. Elizabeth knew there would be no dancing or music as Harriet had when she got married seven years earlier. Mary said she did not mind. She was grateful John wanted to marry her. There was no way she could care for her younger sister and the farm by herself.

John went to San Felipe de Austin to make the arrangements. Mary took her mother's blue wedding dress from the family trunk and tried it on. With a few changes, Elizabeth assured her it would be a perfect dress for the wedding.

The following Monday the *alcalde* and a few personal friends watched Mary and John mark their "X" on the marriage bond. After the simple ceremony, Elizabeth rode home with Harriet so the newlyweds could be alone.

With two happy children underfoot, Elizabeth had little time to herself. Little Hiram was everywhere at once. Keeping up with him was a job. If Hiram was not teasing one of the dogs, he was chasing his mother's chickens, or racing toward the river as fast as his chubby legs would go. His five-year-old brother Elisha was usually not far behind.

During the day, Elizabeth had no time for tears. At night, she was too tired to cry.

Many evenings after supper, William saddled up two horses. With the afternoon sun low in the west, they headed for the peaceful spot William had found. They rode past the vine-covered bushes and thicket of trees draped with Spanish moss. They stopped at the open space not far from Mill Creek. Sitting quietly on a dead

There was a huge panther on the branch directly in front of Elizabeth.

log, a chorus of frogs and twittering birds serenaded them. From the creek came the gurgling sound of water trickling over the rocks. It was at those moments near the end of day that Elizabeth thought of her father. She could almost hear him saying, "When a day's work is done, a fellow can rest knowing he has done his best."

Heading homeward one evening, Elizabeth was in the lead. She neared the place where the path narrowed, twisting its way through the moss-covered trees. The rays of the setting sun were dancing playfully across the bushes beside the trail.

As she neared one of the larger trees, she heard a noise. Sensing danger, she looked around slowly. A chill ran up her spine. There was a huge panther on the branch directly in front of her! It was poised to leap. Elizabeth's heart skipped a beat. Suddenly, the peaceful silence was broken. The panther snarled. Elizabeth screamed. A bullet from William's gun whizzed through the air. She felt the creature brush against her arm. Everything went black.

The next thing she knew, William was patting her cheek. He was kneeling on the ground beside her. "Betsy, speak to me. Speak to me. Tell me you are all right."

Elizabeth nodded her head as she tried to sit up. "I'm all right, but how did I get down here?"

"You fell from your horse when you fainted! You are lucky, Betsy. Panthers are dangerous!" He brushed the dirt from her hair as he helped her to her feet. "If you are sure you are not hurt, let's go home. I want Pa to help me skin that panther before it gets dark. Just look at the size of that critter! I'll bet that hide is worth plenty."

Elizabeth stared at the animal and shuddered. She had come so close to death. She owed her life to William and his keen marksmanship.

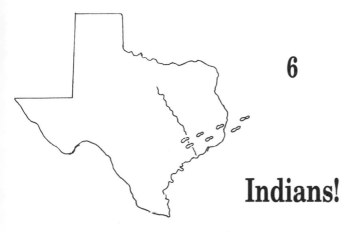

6

Indians!

It was no secret that Elizabeth was afraid of wild animals and Indians. The tales she heard about Indians made her blood run cold.

There was the story of Thomas Thompson. In the summer of 1829 he had returned to find Indians ransacking his home. Mr. Thompson rode for help. He and his neighbors eventually chased the Indians away after a long search.

William's father told the story of a hunter who chanced upon an Indian party camped in a deep ravine near Caney Creek. The hunter slipped away without being seen. When he returned with help, several Indians were wounded before they got away.

Everyone said the Apaches, Comanches, and Karankawas were the most dangerous. Indians had always been a constant threat to the settlers along the Colorado and Brazos rivers. The settlers were warned to stay on the alert. Indians were causing more and more trouble.

Early one morning the dogs started barking as two

riders approached the house. William and his father grabbed their guns and stepped onto the porch just as Churchill Fulshear and his brother galloped into the yard. Elizabeth and Harriet peered at them through the kitchen window.

"What's wrong?" William asked, lowering his gun.

"Injuns! Over at the San Pierre place! They are demanding his corn," Churchill replied angrily. Joseph San Pierre raised the best corn crop of all their neighbors. The man was known for his bull-dog determination to fight for his rights. "Come on! He needs help," Churchill cried.

"We are coming!" Noel shouted as he and the boys ran for their horses. "Harriet, you'd better tie up those dogs or they will follow us. We don't need them causing trouble. You two girls stay inside 'til we get back."

Harriet tied Tex and the other dogs to the porch. Once the men were gone, she bolted the windows and doors. She and Elizabeth loaded their guns and waited. They had not waited long when they heard shots in the distance. Harriet and Elizabeth poked the barrels of their guns through the holes on either side of the window. The dogs barked and growled angrily as two Indian braves appeared in sight.

"Wait until they get closer, Betsy. Don't waste your bullets. It takes time to reload."

The dogs strained at the ropes and growled as the braves neared the house. "Get ready," Harriet whispered. Elizabeth could scarcely breathe. "FIRE!"

Both guns exploded at once. The nearest Indian dropped his bow and arrow. He grabbed his arm and wheeled his horse around to head for the woods. The other Indian was right behind him. Suddenly, a volley of shots was heard nearby. William and his father raced toward the house.

Noel paused long enough to shout, "Is everybody all right in there?"

"We are fine."

With that, Noel and his son dashed off into the woods after the Indians.

The sun was low in the sky when they returned. After supper, the family sat around the table. Harriet and Elizabeth were eager to hear of their adventure.

"I reckon those Indians weren't looking for trouble when they demanded Joseph San Pierre's corn," Noel chuckled. "But when Joseph refused to give it up, the chief got angry. He threatened to kill Joseph and his wife, but Joseph grabbed his gun before anything happened. All the time Mrs. San Pierre was pleading with her husband to give up the corn. The old man held his ground. The chief and his braves finally left, but they set up camp a short distance from the house."

"Yep," Josiah spoke up as his father paused, "that's when the San Pierre boy sneaked out to the neighbors."

William nodded. "We got there just in time. Those Indians were ready to attack. I reckon we surprised that bunch. We wounded some of them before they got away."

Noel looked from his wife to Elizabeth. "I guess we will never know which of you hit that Indian. But one of you is a mighty good shot."

Harriet spoke up. "It was Betsy. I was aiming at the other Indian."

"I always said you would make a good hunter, Betsy," William chuckled.

"But I don't want to be a hunter! Say, what kind of Indians were those anyway?"

"I'm not sure. They weren't Karankawas. They live down on the coast. Karankawas are the ones who cover their bodies with alligator grease to keep away the mosquitoes."

"Yep," Josiah nodded, holding his nose, "you can smell that stuff a mile away. It stinks!"

Elizabeth wondered which was worse — the awful-smelling grease or the itching bite of the mosquitoes.

That winter passed quickly. With the coming of

spring, Elizabeth and William found time to resume their rides. Mounting their horses one day, they rode to their favorite spot. Tex darted in and out of the weeds in front of them. They tied their horses to a tree and sat down on the log.

After talking for a few minutes, they lapsed into silence. William was absorbed in thought as he patted his dog. Elizabeth looked at the flowers. The fields along the creek looked like a patchwork quilt. Indian paintbrushes and winecups were sprinkled among the bluebonnets.

Elizabeth studied the trees. She had never realized leaves could have so many different colors of green and be so different in shape. Even the bark of the trees were not the same.

Her eyes wandered to William. How handsome he was with his coal black hair and sun-tanned skin. How brave and strong he appeared. He had his father's mischievous smile. There was usually a devilish twinkle in his dark eyes. But not today.

"Betsy," William said, straightening his broad shoulders. Once he started talking, the words seemed to leap from his lips. "Betsy, I have something to ask you. Will you marry me? I love you. I love you with all my heart."

A rosy glow swept over Elizabeth's face. She made no sound.

William spoke with an adoring tenderness in his voice. "I've loved you since that day the horse ran away with you. Remember that day?"

She smiled. "But that was seven years ago. I was only eight."

"And I was thirteen. Oh, Betsy, you are so beautiful." When the color deepened in her cheeks he changed his tone. "I have talked to Harriet. We have her blessings. And Pa's too. He is giving us his old wagon and two of his younger oxen — the ones he calls Job and Lot. Pa said I could have one-fourth of the cotton if I go on working in the fields.

"I reckon Pa's looking forward to grandchildren. He sure seems eager to get us married. He said he is giving us this land here along Mill Creek. He and Josiah think we ought to build over there on that ridge. You remember — the water never did get that high during the flood last June. Churchill and his brother are coming over next week to help clear out that underbrush. With luck, we should have the house finished before summer comes." William stopped to get his breath.

"William Roberts! Do you mean you have talked to everybody? Everybody but me?"

"Aw, Betsy," he grinned sheepishly, "haven't you always known we would get married? Everyone else knew."

Elizabeth lifted her chin proudly. "Well, it is nice to be asked. And, if you want to know my answer, it is yes. I will marry you and —"

William had her in his arms before she could finish the sentence.

After that, their plans moved quickly. William and the others started on the cabin once the land was cleared. William insisted Elizabeth go to visit her sister Mary. He wanted the house to be a surprise. When Elizabeth got home, Mary talked about making a new wedding dress for her.

"No, I want to wear Mama's," Elizabeth declared firmly. "It is part of our family. Mama wore that dress when she married Papa. Harriet wore it seven years ago, and you wore it last fall. I want my turn. Who knows, someday your daughter — or mine — may wear that dress. Besides," her eyes grew misty, "Papa would want me to."

"You are right. I am only sorry Papa won't be here to see you." Mary sighed. "John and I want to give you the best wedding we can, Betsy. Since we didn't have a party, we are pretending this is ours too. I hope you don't mind."

"Oh, Mary," Elizabeth cried, throwing her arms around her sister. She had never considered Mary's feelings about not having a fancy wedding and party. How selfish I have been, she thought.

People for miles around San Felipe were invited to the wedding. Elizabeth never knew that time could pass so quickly when there was work to do. A few days before the wedding, Noel took Harriet and the children over to Mary's in the wagon. William and Josiah would not come until later. Elizabeth was grateful that Harriet wanted to iron the blue dress herself. She wanted each fold and tuck to be perfect. The night before the wedding, Harriet brushed and combed Elizabeth's hair until every curl fell into place.

Rex started barking soon after breakfast the next morning. John and Noel ran out to greet the guests who were arriving. Some brought gifts of honey and pecans. Others brought seeds and pieces of lace and ribbon for the bride. William and his brother rode up with Churchill and his family.

By noon the yard was full of wagons. Mary knew the cabin was too small for all the guests. She had the tables moved out under the trees, where it would be cooler. The ceremony would be performed on the porch. Later, they would dance out there.

The women busied themselves arranging the food. The men stood around the fire admiring the roasting turkey and meat. The children managed to get into everyone's way.

Some of the older boys headed to the river with their fishing poles. They took turns cleaning the fish and rolling them in mud after wrapping the fish in leaves. The mud would keep the fish from burning while it cooked with the corn in the hot coals. Roasted fish and corn were favorites with everybody.

While the guests were visiting, Elizabeth's sisters helped her into her dress. Mary smoothed the folds in Elizabeth's skirts as Harriet pinned a wreath of wildflowers in her hair. They assured Elizabeth she was as pretty as a picture.

Once Elizabeth was ready, William's father stepped to the center of the porch. With a booming voice he said, "Friends." He waited. A hush fell upon the crowd. "We have gathered here to join my son William Roberts and Elizabeth Pryor in holy matrimony. Judge Robert Peebles and Isaac Pennington will conduct the services. Betsy, you and William join hands. Churchill Fulshear, Edward Coty, and Efram Williams will act as witnesses."

The guests watched quietly as the bride and groom exchanged their vows. Then the couple made their "X" upon the marriage bond. Someone cried, "Hey, William, let's see you kiss your wife!"

After the kiss the noise of the shivaree began. Elizabeth had only vague memories of the dance and all that happened after that. It was like a dream. Not until William stopped the wagon in front of their beautiful new home the next morning did Elizabeth realize she was now Mrs. William Roberts!

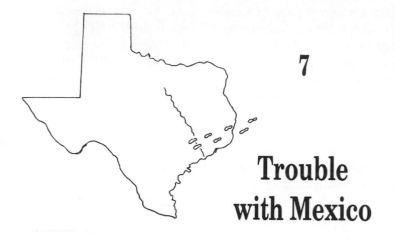

7

Trouble
with Mexico

Elizabeth never imagined she could be so happy to
have a home of her own. They had been married about a
week when she said, "Oh, William, the cabin is more
than I ever dreamed it could be!"

"Pa always says if you do a thing, do it right the first
time," William said as he looked around the room.
"There is still lots to do. We could use some more chairs
or maybe a bench or two for when we have company. It
might be nice if we had a cupboard like Pa made for Harriet. You could put your dishes and others things in it.
But first, I want to put a shelf above the fireplace. Then I
will make a couple of racks for our guns. There will be
plenty to do in the evenings when I come in from the
field."

The couple spent their evenings working together.
Harriet had given Elizabeth enough calico to make a
dress. Elizabeth decided they needed ruffled curtains for
the six windows more than she needed a new dress. She
sewed on those while William made the shelves.

One morning they planted the seeds Mary had given them. William carried water from the creek to be sure the seeds would grow. Elizabeth looked forward to having a garden of her own.

Toward the end of September, William started talking about having a party and inviting all their neighbors. "I sure would like for folks to see our house now that it's almost finished. But if we give a party it ought to be before the fall rains set in."

Elizabeth agreed. They decided October 27 would be a good day. That would be Elizabeth's sixteenth birthday. William wanted to make it a birthday she would never forget. Everyone he invited knew it was going to be a surprise birthday party for Elizabeth. Noel asked the musicians to play so everyone could dance. Unknown to William, Noel and Harriet had a special gift for Elizabeth.

By noon, the day of the party, the neighbors began arriving. First came the Thomas Westalls, then David Randon and his wife. The Fulshears and the Penningtons and the Brookshires arrived a short time later. Elizabeth's sister Mary and her husband John Hensley came next. Some of the guests brought along baskets of baked fish and corn as well as other things to eat. When everybody was there and all was ready, William shouted, "Happy Birthday, Betsy!"

"Happy Birthday, Elizabeth!" everyone cried. She was too surprised to speak.

On a signal from his father, Josiah appeared around the corner of the house. He was leading Old Red. Noel put his arm around Elizabeth. "Betsy, I once told you I wanted a pretty blue-eyed daughter of my own. Now I have one! Your sister and I want you to have a horse of your own so you can come and visit us anytime you wish." He put the reins to Old Red into Elizabeth's hand.

"Oh, Pa," she cried, throwing her arms around Noel's neck. "Harriet is right — you are wonderful!"

Her father-in-law threw back his head and laughed. Everyone joined in.

"Now," Noel declared as the laughter died down, "I'm hungry! Let's eat!"

The guests moved toward the table laden with food. Once their plates were full, they moved aside to find a place to sit. While the women exchanged recipes the men talked about the weather and their crops. Soon the music began. The dancers moved to the porch between the two cabins. They stomped and clapped, and clapped and stomped. The music went on for hours.

The sun was peeking up over the trees when the party came to an end. With loud farewells the guests hitched their horses to their wagons and headed home. Elizabeth's birthday party had been a big success. Even Josiah agreed.

The spring of 1835 came and went. Elizabeth would not have been so happy had she realized trouble was brewing between the Mexican government and the settlers. She had no way of knowing that at the town of Anahuac a force of Mexican soldiers marched in, demanding payment of taxes. The people of the town refused to pay the customs tax on goods brought into or leaving the country. The soldiers became angry. They arrested some of the citizens and put them into jail.

When William Travis learned of the problem at Anahuac, he went there with a group of men to see what could be done. The soldiers finally agreed to release their prisoners. An uneasy calm settled over the town.

When Stephen Austin returned to San Felipe in July 1835, the news spread quickly. His friends were shocked by the change in him. The months in the Mexican jail had not treated him kindly. He had a hacking cough which racked his thin, frail body.

All of the settlers in Texas liked and respected Stephen Austin. They asked his advice about paying the customs tax. Austin told them to accept Santa Anna's laws or be prepared to fight.

Elizabeth listened to Noel and the other men talk.

When she was alone with William she shook her head and said, "There is going to be trouble."

"Now, honey," William teased, "you are just nervous because you are going to have a baby."

"No, it isn't that," she protested. "There will be trouble. I just know it."

By the first of October, William knew she was right. He was working near the house one morning when he saw his friend Benjamin Fulcher ride into the yard. He ran over to greet him as Elizabeth stepped out the door. William could see he was in a hurry.

"Is something wrong, Ben?"

"What is it?" Elizabeth demanded nervously.

"Haven't you heard?" Benjamin did not wait for their answer. "Five of General Cos's Mexican soldiers from San Antonio rode into Gonzales. They demanded the return of the cannon the government gave the town to use as protection against the Indians. The folks of Gonzales refused to give up their cannon. When some of the fellows of San Felipe heard Gonzales needed help, they left at once.

"I understand Stephen Austin is asking for volunteers to go with him. They'll be leaving in the morning. My brother Graves and I are going. We figured you might want to come along, William. We feel it's our duty to help our neighbors."

William ran his fingers through his dark hair. "We will see, Ben. If I am not at your place by sunup, don't wait for me. We will talk about it. You understand." He rolled his eyes in Elizabeth's direction. Benjamin nodded and, wheeling his horse around, waved goodbye as he galloped away.

Elizabeth and William discussed the matter. She knew he wanted to go but was reluctant to leave her alone. She said, "Honey, you should go. Ben was right. It is our duty. I can stay with Pa and Harriet until you get back. I will be all right."

"Are you sure?"

49

She laughed. "Of course. The baby is not due for almost four months. This is only October."

"Don't worry," William said grimly, "I will be home before January. I reckon I had better ride over and tell Pa goodbye."

The next morning the couple were up before daybreak. William tied his bedroll to his saddle and looked down at Elizabeth. "Honey, no need for you to rush. I told your sister you would be there sometime before noon. Take your time. Take care of yourself while I am gone." He kissed her and got up on his horse. And with a wave of his hand, he rode away.

Elizabeth brushed a tear from her cheek as she walked into the house. She busied herself putting things in place. The cabin seemed strangely silent as she gathered up her clothes to take to Harriet's.

In the days that followed, Elizabeth had little time to worry. Between the children and the dogs bringing in the mud from the yard, the housework was never done.

William had been gone several weeks when fifty-eight delegates from the other settlements met at San Felipe. At the meeting the delegates talked about the pros and cons of declaring independence from Mexico. The men could not agree. It was finally decided that until Mexico's President Santa Anna abided by the Constitution of 1824, they did have the right to govern themselves. Although they were loyal citizens of Mexico, they had a right to take up arms for protection.

They voted to send Stephen Austin to the States to ask for money for supplies and to ask for men to come to Texas. The delegates adjourned on November 14. They would meet again in March of 1836 at the town of Washington-on-the-Brazos.

As the weeks slipped by, some of the volunteers returned. They said Austin and his men had followed the Mexican soldiers from Gonzales on to San Antonio. Austin had hoped that General Cos would run out of supplies and then surrender. He set up camp to wait. The weather

50

turned cold and wet. A few of the volunteers grew tired of waiting. They decided to go home where it was warm.

November came and went. By the second week in December, Elizabeth began to worry. Had something happened to William? What if he did not get home in time for the baby?

A fine mist was falling one afternoon when the dogs started barking. The children squealed as they ran toward the door. Elizabeth and her sister were not far behind. They saw a lone rider coming down the trail. As he rode nearer, Elizabeth cried, "It's William! He's home! He's home at last!"

The family gathered around the long table in Noel's kitchen. At first everyone talked at once. It was difficult for William to answer their questions. They wanted to hear his story. He finally told them to be quiet and he would start at the beginning. He had been with Stephen Austin as they rode to the edge of San Antonio and set up camp. When Austin left for the States, Colonel Edward Burleson had taken over the command. They still hoped General Cos would surrender without a fight.

William confessed he had grown tired of being cold and hungry during those weeks of waiting. He had been tempted to abandon the group and come home. But when Ben Milam said, "Who will go with Old Ben?" William had stepped forward with 300 other volunteers. On the third day of battle he had been near Milam when he was killed. After that, William said they fought from house to house to force the enemy to the old deserted mission called the Alamo.

On December 9, General Cos surrendered. Colonel Burleson sent part of his troops to escort the Mexican soldiers to the Rio Grande to be sure they returned to Mexico. The rest of the Texans went home. William was proud to say that in the four-day battle of the Siege of Bexar, 300 Texans had defeated a force of some 1,300 soldiers. Everyone agreed they did a good job.

William sighed as he finished his story. "It is good to

be back. Come on, Betsy, get your things. Let's go home." Elizabeth loved being with her sister's family but she was eager to get to her home.

A cold and sharp north wind blew in the first days of January. Elizabeth's sister Mary decided she would come and stay until the baby arrived. She knew Elizabeth would need help. The nearest doctor was in San Felipe, and the road was knee-deep in mud. William would never be able to get to town and back with the doctor in time.

Early one morning, Elizabeth moaned. William's eyes popped open as she whispered, "Honey . . . Get Mary . . . Hurry!"

William sprang out of bed and lighted the lamp. He jumped into his pants as he ran to the adjoining room for Mary. She heard him coming and grabbed her dress. With her shoes in her hands she ran back to take a look at Elizabeth. "Build us a big fire in here, then put on plenty of water to heat, William. After you have done that, get out."

William spent the rest of the morning pacing the floor, staring at the door Mary had shut in his face. The sun was directly overhead when William heard a baby cry. He pressed his ear against the door, fighting the urge to run into the room. He gritted his teeth and, with his hands clasped behind his back, paced the floor some more. William felt sure time had stopped.

Finally, Mary opened the door with a weary smile on her face. "You may come in now."

"Honey," Elizabeth whispered softly from the bed in the corner of the room. "Come see your son — Churchill Roberts."

William wanted to shout for joy but grinned from ear to ear instead. He was speechless. They had already planned to name the baby after William's best friend if it was a boy. William knelt beside the bed. He kissed Elizabeth on the cheek and took a closer look at the tiny bundle nestled in her arm. William never knew anything so red and little could be so beautiful!

8

"Santa Anna's Coming!"

In the days that followed, Elizabeth was too busy to think of anything but the baby. Yet, miles away in San Antonio, events were taking place which would change her life.

At the Alamo, Colonel William Travis and James Bowie had joined Colonel J. C. Neill and his men. When Neill left, the two men shared the command. But then James Bowie became ill, and Travis assumed command. After Davy Crockett and his volunteers from Tennessee arrived, there were some 150 men.

The lookout in the old church tower sounded the warning on the morning of February 23. Santa Anna was coming! Travis ordered his troops inside the walls of the Alamo and sent for help. He needed reinforcements and ammunition. Only thirty-two men from Gonzales answered his call. Travis was forced to defend the old mission with 189 men.

On the morning of March 6, the enemy made its final

assault. In about ninety minutes, the battle was over. The Alamo had fallen.

Travis died without knowing that four days earlier, at Washington-on-the-Brazos, delegates had signed Texas's Declaration of Independence from Mexico. Sam Houston was appointed commander of the new Texan army. With the talk of war, many of the settlers began packing their wagons to leave. They feared there was no way General Houston could stop Santa Anna with so few men.

One morning, Tex barked wildly as a wagon rumbled into the yard. Elizabeth peered out the window and saw John Hensley and her sister Mary.

"Hush, Tex. We have enough trouble," John scolded as he jumped from the wagon and ran into the kitchen. "Get your things! Hurry! The Alamo has fallen! Santa Anna is marching his troops through Texas and says that he will take no prisoners! General Houston has sent word that the Mexican army is coming this way."

John glanced in William's direction. "While I help the women, you get your horses, William. You can ride in front of us. Tie your other horses to the wagon with mine. If you leave them, the soldiers will get them when they come this way. I stopped by Noel's house to warn them. Harriet said they would go on ahead. We can catch up with them down the road. Get your oxen — they can help mine pull the wagon. They may be slow, but they are strong. Hurry!"

William dashed out the door while John helped load the wagon. By the time William returned with the horses and oxen, Elizabeth and the baby were already in the back of the wagon. Mary was on the seat. William tied his horses to the back of the wagon and hitched his oxen to the front.

"Let's go!" John shouted, goading the oxen to hurry them along. With that, they were off.

By the time they reached the main road, it was jammed with wagons. Some of the wagons were so crowded with household goods that the women and children had to walk. Most of the younger men had gone to join General Houston. Only a few older ones remained. Panic filled the air.

William rode ahead to find his father. He came back a short time later and said that they would make camp before dark. They would try to bring the two wagons together then. With so many people it would be useless to try before evening. William told Elizabeth that Josiah had gone with the Fulshears to join the Texan army. From the look on his face, she knew William wanted to be there too.

He peered into the wagon. "Are you and the baby all right, Betsy?"

She smiled bravely. "We are fine. Don't worry about us."

By late afternoon everyone was tired and hungry. John saw Noel's wagon up ahead and they soon set up camp for the night under a large oak tree. In their hasty departure, some of the women had not had time to think of food. They had little or nothing to eat. Noel remembered to get a coffee pot, and Harriet had packed plenty of coffee. William and John managed to shoot a deer while the others built a fire and made the coffee. The pungent aroma of roasting meat lifted everyone's spirits. After a hot meal, they all felt better.

The men kept the fire burning as they took turns standing guard that night. Aside from the howl of a coyote and the screech of an owl, Elizabeth heard nothing unusual. She and Mary curled up in the back of the wagon with the baby between them.

After a hurried breakfast the next morning, the group started out again. Noel moved out first. John pulled his wagon right behind. They had not gone far when a fine mist began to fall. Mary crawled under the cover of the wagon so she would not get wet. The road grew rough and bumpy with so many wagons. The

A constant stream of riders passed them. Their warning was always the same. "Hurry! Santa Anna is coming!"

wheels gouged deep ruts into the soft dirt. And now the steady drizzle turned the dirt into mud. Travel was slow.

A constant stream of riders passed them. Their warning was always the same. "Hurry! Santa Anna is coming!"

The drizzle turned into a light rain. Every few miles they passed a deserted house. Stopping at one they found the door ajar, beds unmade, and the dishes left on the table. In the yard were a number of hungry chickens and a forlorn-looking dog. Elizabeth fought back the tears. She thought of Rex and Tex and the other dogs back home. John said that there was no way they could bring them. The dogs might be lonely, but they would not go hungry. They were good hunters and would find something to eat. Elizabeth hoped that John was right.

"Why don't we move out alone?" Mary asked when they made camp.

"It would not be safe for one or two families to travel alone. What if the Indians decided to attack? Or if Santa Anna's men caught them alone — what could they do? No. There is safety in numbers. We may travel slowly, but we will all stay together," Noel replied.

The next morning they passed a number of wagons that had broken down. Household possessions were scattered along the way where people had abandoned them, unable to carry them any further. As far as Elizabeth could see, the roads were clogged with wagons and carts of every description and size. The scene was one of despair.

Elizabeth tried to shut out the world by looking at her baby's soft, cuddly face. Even at his young age Churchill looked much like William and his father. He was going to have the same black hair and olive-colored skin. Elizabeth felt sure that his eyes were getting darker too. How wonderful it was that Churchill was content to eat and sleep, never knowing that their world was crumbling around them.

Harriet was not so fortunate. Elisha and Hiram were

57

difficult to manage. Hiram had thought the wagon ride was a game at first. It had not taken the boy long to change his mind. Hiram wanted down to run and play. He kept crying for his dogs. It took force to keep the children in the wagon. Mary could see her sister needed help. Harriet was completely exhausted.

Elizabeth lost track of time. The days merged one into another. One evening William talked to a woman with her five children in the wagon beside them. The lady said that her husband, Henry Jones, was in the back of their wagon. He had been ill for some time. Mrs. Jones and her two older boys took turns driving the wagon. William told Mrs. Jones to call him if she needed help. Elizabeth fell asleep remembering Papa's words, "No matter how bad times are, they can always get worse."

Thinking of Mrs. Jones and her problems made Elizabeth wonder what was going to happen. She knew Noel was worrying about getting Harriet and the boys to safety. What about Mary? John had kissed her goodbye and ridden off to join General Houston. Elizabeth knew William would be leaving soon. She made up her mind that she would not let him go without her. His fate would be her fate. Elizabeth decided to say nothing of her decision until it was time.

"The roads seem to be getting worse. They are almost impassable in places," William complained one afternoon as he drove the wagon. Suddenly, there was a splintery, cracking sound. The wagon groaned as it tilted to one side and stopped. William and his father inspected the damage. The axle was broken. The wagon was beyond repair. There was nothing to do but abandon it.

Elizabeth was told to take only what she needed. They must leave the rest. She made a bundle of what she could carry while William hitched his and John's oxen to his father's wagon. They agreed the extra oxen would be needed if the mud got deeper.

"Betsy, I have something to tell you," William said as he rubbed a spot of mud from her cheek. "You must go on with Pa. It is time I joined Josiah and the others. It is my duty."

A slow-burning fire glowed in her eyes as Elizabeth straightened her shoulders. "Don't you say a word. I have made up my mind, William. We are going with you! I can stay with the women following General Houston's men." When he tried to protest, she shook her head. "No, it will do no good. Don't you understand? I lost my mama. I lost my papa. But I am not losing you — not if I can help it, William Roberts! The baby and I are going with you. The matter is settled."

No amount of arguing would make her change her mind. She would not listen to her sisters or Noel. With tears of farewell, Elizabeth clutched her baby to her bosom as she mounted Old Red to follow her husband.

They had not traveled far when they met with others joining Houston's troops. Near Groce's Crossing they came to the women and children camped a short distance from Houston's men. William left Elizabeth with the women and rode ahead to find his brother.

He did not have to search long. Josiah and John were among the group, cleaning their guns and sharpening their knives. The next morning William and his brother were ordered to join Colonel Sidney Sherman's sixty-horse cavalry unit. They spent the day patrolling the woods looking for Mexican soldiers. It was almost dark when they returned to camp, tired and hungry. They found that there was plenty of boiled meat and corn from the Groce plantation. That night, William fell asleep worrying about Elizabeth and the baby.

Early the next morning Houston gave the order to move out. A scout reported that the Mexican army was not far away. Santa Anna and some 750 men were at the town of Harrisburg.

The rain-soaked earth made movement slow. The Texans soon saw a column of smoke rising in the southern sky. Santa Anna was burning Harrisburg.

When the settlers reached Buffalo Bayou, they hurriedly built rafts to carry them across the marshy bayou. Once they were on the opposite bank, they rested in the woods until dark. Under the cloak of night they were ordered to go on.

After crossing the wooden bridge over Vince's Bayou, the Texans paused briefly. The next morning they took control of Lynch's Ferry on the San Jacinto River. A short distance away, Santa Anna's men were burning the town of New Washington. With the town ablaze, the Mexican soldiers marched toward Lynch's Ferry to face General Sam Houston and his troops.

In the woods, the Texans took up their position with their twin cannons. As they waited for the enemy, William could see smoke from a town burning in the distance. He looked around to get his bearings. The prairie in front of him was covered with high grass. William noticed a line of liveoak trees covered with strands of Spanish moss behind him. On his right was Buffalo Bayou. The banks of the bayou were partly hidden by a thicket of trees. The San Jacinto River and Lynch's Ferry were on William's left.

The Mexican army reached the river before nightfall and set up camp about a mile away from the Texan camp. A brief exchange of bullets followed. Both sides soon discovered the distance between them was too great. It was foolish to waste the ammunition.

While William and the other Texans settled for the night, reinforcements arrived in the enemy's camp. After their long, hard march the Mexican soldiers were tired. The next morning all was quiet in both camps. Each side waited for the other to make a move. Neither did. That afternoon Santa Anna's men were allowed to rest. During the enemy's *siesta,* the Texans received orders to prepare for battle. They wasted no time loading their guns. They were ready to fight!

General Houston commanded his army to move silently across the prairie toward Santa Anna's camp. William and the others in Colonel Sherman's cavalry unit hid among the trees, waiting for orders to charge. At the proper moment General Houston waved his battered hat. On that signal the foot soldiers leaped forward shouting, "Remember the Alamo!"

At that moment William's group dashed from the trees. Colonel Sherman cried, "Let's go!" The Mexican camp was slowly coming to life. The sleepy-eyed soldiers stumbled from their tents, waving their guns and screaming, "Me no Alamo!"

William and his brother were side by side with their rifles ready to fire as they neared the camp. William saw a Mexican soldier with a bayonet, crouched and waiting for Josiah as he rode past. William dashed ahead and fired. The soldier screamed and slumped to the ground.

Before they reached the enemy camp one of the Texans, Deaf Smith, yelled, "Vince's Bridge is down. Fight! Fight for your lives, boys!"

"Victory is certain," General Houston shouted as a storm of bullets whizzed through the air. The general grabbed his leg. His horse collapsed under him. Both had been shot. In the confusion, someone grabbed one of the riderless horses for the general. He remounted, grimacing with the pain of his wounded leg.

"Spread out, men," Colonel Sherman cried. William and his unit moved quickly around the camp. The Texans had swooped down upon Santa Anna's troops with lightning speed. The Mexican cannoneers were unable to reach their cannon in time to fire. Many dropped their guns as they ran toward the woods to find cover. William and his unit rode after them. The Mexicans found there was no way to escape. They lifted their arms, again crying, "Me no Alamo!" Santa Anna's army surrendered.

The battle was over. Texas was free!

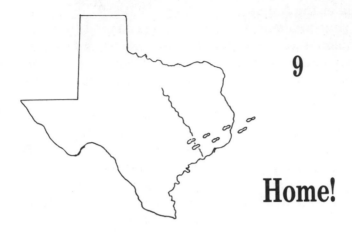

9

Home!

"Oh, William," Elizabeth cried, with tears streaming down her cheeks. "Is it over? Is it really over?"

"Yes, the battle is over. Texas is free. Come on. Let's go." William reached for the baby. "I'll carry him. You had better lift your skirts, Betsy, and watch your step."

Zig-zagging around the dead and dying on the battlefield, Elizabeth felt faint from the sight of blood and the stench of death. She would never have believed how quickly it all happened had she not been so near San Jacinto. William and Josiah headed toward the large tree in the distance. Elizabeth saw a man with a wounded leg propped against the tree. She did not recognize General Sam Houston at first. His face was lined and pinched with pain.

"Sir," William said respectfully, "may I speak to you?"

The general nodded.

"My name is William Roberts and this is my brother

Josiah. If you do not need us any longer, sir, my brother and I would like permission to go home."

The general's weary face softened. He looked from the baby to Elizabeth as he said, "Take your family home, son. This is no place for them. The others can clean up this mess. You are dismissed, soldiers. Thank you for your service to Texas."

"Thank you, sir," William said proudly. "Come along, Betsy." He helped her onto Old Red and handed her the baby. The three rode across the fields, avoiding the muddy trail. That night they stopped before dark. William hobbled the horses so they could graze. Josiah gathered wood and started a fire. The two men rested with their guns in their arms as Elizabeth and the baby slept at their feet. At the first light of day, they started out again.

Elizabeth wondered if they would ever get home. What would they find? Her spirits lifted when they met some of their neighbors. Over and over she asked each newcomer if they had seen Noel and her sisters. The answer was always the same as they shook their heads sadly. Elizabeth tried not to worry. Surely Harriet and Mary were safe, but where could they be?

Faces were grim as they talked of the soldiers who had burned and ransacked everything in their path. Elizabeth knew the towns of Harrisburg, Gonzales, and San Felipe were in ashes. Had the enemy destroyed everything?

William and Josiah rode ahead as they neared their father's place. They stopped on top of the last hill. Their worst fears were true. The house was gone. Only the chimney remained. A few stalks of corn were still standing.

"Come on. There is nothing we can do here," William looked grim. "It isn't much farther. We might as well find out the worst."

"Yep!" Josiah agreed.

Tears of exhaustion and grief trickled down Eliza-

Tex ran to welcome them.

beth's cheeks as they traveled the old familiar path. At the thicket she glanced up to the branch of the old oak tree. The day the panther had attacked her seemed a lifetime ago. After San Jacinto, that animal seemed like a kitten.

Elizabeth's heart beat wildly. She was afraid to look as they neared the clearing.

William, riding ahead, suddenly gave a whoop. "Betsy, Josiah, look!" Elizabeth could only stare in disbelief. The house was untouched! It was just the way they had left it. The vegetables in the garden seemed to be welcoming them home.

"But how?" she muttered feebly as William helped her to the ground.

"I don't know. Maybe the Mexican soldiers didn't come back this far. They were following the river, and I guess they couldn't see our house back here behind the trees. I am glad I never got around to cutting them down. As far as I am concerned, those trees can stay forever." Elizabeth sank to the ground on her knees.

Suddenly, a black and white streak came running toward them. Tex barked joyously as he put his paws on William's stomach. Then he ran to Elizabeth to lick her face and the baby's with his warm, moist tongue. Seeing Josiah standing nearby, the dog ran to lick his hand.

"He seems almost as glad to have us home as we are to be home," William sighed wearily.

Elizabeth rocked back on her heels and sobbed with tears of joy. "It is over! It's really over!"

Before the week ended, Mary and John returned with Harriet and her family. John had chanced upon Noel and his wagon when he headed homeward.

Once they were together, everyone talked at once. Elizabeth insisted that Harriet stay with them while William and Josiah helped their father rebuild. There were vegetables in the garden and fresh sweet corn in the field. They would not go hungry. Mary and her husband decided to go home. They wanted to see what was left of their place. They would face it together.

Noel and his sons worked hard. They had the new cabin built in no time. Thoughts of war gradually faded.

Folks were talking about General Sam Houston. He was elected the first president of the new Republic of Texas. Stephen Austin was appointed secretary of state. The town of Columbia became the capital.

Austin took his job seriously. He worked for three days and nights to complete a report in his cold, partly furnished room. Everyone knew Austin had never fully recovered from the hardships he had suffered while in the Mexican prison. In his weakened condition, and working without a fire, he became ill and developed pneumonia. Stephen Austin died on December 27, 1836.

Elizabeth had great respect for the kind, gentle man who had brought her family to Texas. It was reported that shortly before his death Austin had said:

> I have no house, no roof in all Texas that I can call my own . . . The only one I had was burned at San Felipe . . . I have no farm, no cotton plantation, no income, no money, no comforts . . . I am still in debt for the expenses of my trips to Mexico in 1833, '34, '35.

Elizabeth regretted that Austin had never married in all his forty-three years. It had been rumored he might marry his cousin, Mary Austin Holley. But that was not to be.

Elizabeth closed her eyes. A gentle breeze blew through the trees. Clasping little Churchill to her bosom, she listened to the squeaky rocker as she rocked back and forth. She thought of all that Texas had given her.

In spite of the hardships and heartaches, life had been good. Her father, William Pryor, along with Noel Roberts and others of the first colony, had carved a new life from an unsettled wilderness. With undaunted courage those brave settlers had faced diseases, floods, wild animals, and savage Indians. In her brief years, she had known men like Stephen Austin and William Barret Travis.

A sense of contentment and peace flooded her soul. With men like Sam Houston, David Burnet, and Mirabeau Lamar in control, the future of Texas looked bright. Whatever lay ahead, Elizabeth was proud she and William had been among those early pioneers who had left their footprints in Texas soil.

Bibliography

Juvenile

Baker, Amy Jo. *Texas Past to Present*. Lexington, Massachusetts: D.C. Heath and Company, 1988.

Grisham, Noel. *Crossroads at San Felipe*. Austin: Eakin Press, 1980.

Pearson, Jim, and Ben Proctor. *Texas: The Land and Its People*. Dallas: Hendrick-Long Publishing Company, 1978.

Adult

Barker, Eugene C. *The Life of Stephen F. Austin*. Austin: University of Texas Press, 1969.

Daughters of the Republic of Texas. *Muster Rolls of the Texas Revolution*. Lubbock, Texas: Craftsman Printers, Inc., 1986.

Deweese, W. B. *Letters From an Early Settler of Texas*. Waco: Texian Press, 1968.

Diary of William Barret Travis: August 30, 1833–June 26, 1834. Waco: Texian Press, 1966.

King, C. Richard, ed. *Victorian Lady on the Texas Frontier*. Norman, Oklahoma: University of Oklahoma Press, 1968.

Miller, Thomas Lloyd. *Bounty and Donation Land Grants of Texas*. Austin: University of Texas Press.

Nevin, David. *The Texans*. New York: Time-Life Books, 1975.

Smithwick, Noah. *The Evolution of a State or Recollections of Old Texas Days*. Austin: University of Texas Press, 1983.

Sowell, A. J. *History of Fort Bend County*. Houston: W. H. Coyle Company, 1904.

Wharton, Clarence. *History of Fort Bend County*. San Antonio: Naylor Company, 1939.

Wilbarger, J. W. *Indian Depredations in Texas*. Austin: Hutchings Printing House, 1889.

Periodicals

"Old Three Hundred, The." *The Quarterly of the Texas State Historical Association*, July 1897.

Rather, Ethel Zivley. "De Witt's Colony." *The Quarterly of the Texas State Historical Association*, October 1904.

Primary Sources

Austin County Records, Bellville, Texas. Marriage bond of Elizabeth Pryor and William Roberts.

Fort Bend County. Succession Records, Probate Court Files.

General Land Office, Austin. Map of original land grants of Fort Bend County.

————. 1828 land grant signed by Stephen Austin.

————. Stephen F. Austin's Register of Families.

State of Texas Federal Population Schedules *Seventh Census of the United States*, 1850 and 1860.

Department of Bexar
Jurisdiction of Austin

Before me Robert Peebles Judge of the
first Instance, Personally Came William Roberts
and Elizabeth Pryor all of whom I know and
to whose acts I give full faith and credit who declare
that the Said William Roberts and Elizabeth Pryor
have agreed to Unite themselves in the holy bands
of Matrimony — And to live together in all things
according to God's holy Ordinance. And seeing as
much as there is in this Jurisdiction No person
legally authorized to Solemnize the Same — and
desirous that the Same Should be made as proper
and binding as the peculiar Circumstances of the
Country will permit. They enter into and Sign
this Instrument of Writing And bind themselves
the one to the other in the Penal Sum of Five
thousand dollars — ~~~~~~~~~~~~~~~
~~~~~~~~~~ Conditioned that if the Said
William Roberts and Elizabeth Pryor Shall
So Soon as any one legally authorized to Solemn
=ize Marriages offers in this Jurisdiction by
which Said Marriage may be legally Solemnized
that the Same Shall take place — And on
the refusal of any one of the Said parties to
perform the Obligation into which by this
Instrument he or She May have entered. Then
the party So refusing Shall be liable to the other
in the full amount of the Penalty into which
by this obligation he or She has entered
This done on the Brazos this 7th day of July
1834 in presence of Isaac M. Pennington
and Moses A Forti — Instrumental Witnesses
and those of my Assistants with whom
I Sign to Authenticate this act —

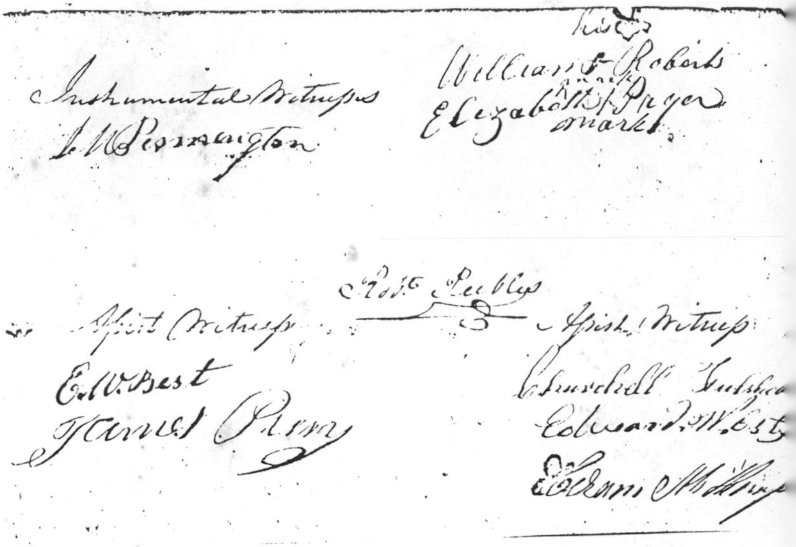

[Handwritten signatures at top of page]

Instrumental Witnesses
I. M. Pennington

his
William + Roberts
Elizabeth + Pryor
mark

Robt. Peebles

First Witness
E. W. Best
James Perry

First Witness
Churchill Fulshear
Edward W. Coty
Efram Williams

MARRIAGE BOND OF THE GREAT-GREAT-GRANDPARENTS OF RITA LEE ROBERTS KERR

Department of Bexar
Jurisdiction of Austin

Before me Robert Peebles Judge of the first instance, Personally came William Roberts and Elizabeth Pryor all of whom I know and to whose acts I give full faith and credit who declare that the said William Roberts and Elizabeth Pryor have agreed to unite themselves in the holy bonds of matrimony — and to live together in all things according to God's holy ordinance — and in as much as there is in this Jurisdiction no person legally authorized to solemnize the same — and desirous that the same should be made as perfect and binding as the peculiar circumstances of the country will permit. They enter into and sign this instrument of writing and bind themselves the one to the other in the Penal sum of Five thousand dollars — conditioned that if the said William Roberts and Elizabeth Pryor shall so soon as any one legally authorized to solemnize marriages offers in this Jurisdiction by which said marriage may be legally solemnized that the same shall take place — and on the refusal of any one of the said parties to perform the obligation into which by this Instrument he or she may have entered, Then the party so refusing shall be liable to the other in the full amount of the Penalty into which by this obligation he or she has entered.

This done on the Brazos this 7th day of July 1834 in presence of Isaac M. Pennington — and Mark A. Forte — Instrumental Witnesses and those of my assistants with whom I sign to authenticate this act.

Instrumental Witnesses:
I. M. Pennington

his
William + Roberts
mark
Elizabeth + Pryor
mark

Robt. Peebles

Asst. Witnesses:
E. W. Best
James Perry

Asst. Witnesses:
Churchill Fulshear
Edward W. Coty
Efram Williams